DO
NARWHALS
HAVE
BLOWHOLES?

Edgar was a bright
and curious young yeti,

But before we follow
their tracks in the snow,
There are a few things about
yetis that you ought to know.

Yetis are huge
and covered in hair,
If you spot one you're lucky,
as they're extremely rare.

But one of the things that you mustn't forget,
Is that no one has met a mean yeti yet.

If you look past all of their threatening features,
You'll discover that yetis are the gentlest creatures.

Edgar was confused by what Freddy said,
So he asked, "What's a narwhal?"
as he scratched his head.
"Narwhals are whales with long, pointy horns,"
Freddy answered with glee,
"You can go ask my mom if you don't believe me!"

This puzzled Edgar and he wasn't sure what to say,
So he blurted out something that is strange to this day.

"Do narwhals have blowholes?" was his curious query,
But neither could come up with a viable theory.

They decided to head toward the Arctic North Pole,
To find out for themselves about the blowhole.

So they gathered their things
with some fruit and some bread,
And quickly jumped onto
the traveling sled.

"To the North!" said Fast Freddy
as they sped down the slope,
Eyes wide with excitement and
gleaming with hope.

They traveled nonstop
through ice storms and blizzards,
They asked for directions
from two battling wizards.

And after seven days of
perpetual motion,
They finally made it to
the Arctic Ocean.

They spent the night
on the snowy beach,
Knowing that the answer
was finally within reach.

The next morning they knew
there was no time to stall,
If they wanted to find
a friendly narwhal.

So they hopped on an iceberg
and floated out to sea,
Hoping to end up
where a narwhal might be.

They continued on
at Fast Freddy's insistence,
Until he suddenly yelled,
"What's that in the distance?"

Out on the horizon
they could see some commotion,
Then a long, pointy horn
emerged from the ocean.

Edgar smiled and said, "We're doing just fine,
But I wonder if you could answer a question of mine?"

"But of course," was the friendly narwhal's reply,
"I might not know the answer, but I'll certainly try."

"Do narwhals have blowholes?" Edgar eagerly inquired,
"We're a long way from home and we're awfully tired."

Then suddenly he said,
"Quick, climb on my back,
We need to get moving
before the lemmings attack!"

So Edgar and Freddy
jumped onto the whale,
And they were gone in a flash
with a flick of his tail.

As they rode on his back
towards the icy seashore,
They both found the answer
they'd been looking for.

The question was answered,
the mystery solved,
Thank goodness the lemmings
were never involved.

Safe on the shore
they said good-bye to their friend,
And with that, this fine story
has come to an end.

Words: Gibson Holub

Pictures: Matt Cory

ISBN-13: 978-1-4196-5487-9
ISBN-10: 1-4196-5487-X

Made in the USA